SOME TALES

Arul Shah

Passionate Player?

As you dive into the pages of this book, get   ready to embark on an exciting journey into the world of Minecraft!

You'll uncover the secrets behind its creatures, and explore the mysteries of its vast and dynamic world.
With every turn of the page, you'll discover
new and fascinating details about this beloved game. So, get ready to join the adventure and become a

Minecraft master
Some Tales Arul Shah

Social Media Handles:

YouTube: Arul Shah(@arulshah)

Instagram: thearulshah

Gmail: notarulshah1104@gmail.com

DEDICATION

This book is dedicated to those passionate Minecraft players who don't just play the game but want to dive it in, explore it and want to solve the most unsolved mysteries of the game.

Share this GREAT book to your friends and family so that everyone

can unreveal the secrets of this
book……

Preface

In Minecraft's world of endless wonder,
There's a mystery that pulls me under.
An enigma shrouded in the game's lore,
A secret that begs to be explored.

I've searched through forests and oceans deep,
Scaled mountains are high and valleys are
steep.
But clues are few and far between,
A puzzle that's yet to be seen.

What lies beyond the game's facade,
Is it treasure, power, or something odd?
Is there a way to unlock the code,
To unravel the secrets, in this world bestowed?

My curiosity is peaked, my mind ablaze,
With theories and ideas, I'm lost in a maze.
But one thing's for sure, I won't give up,
Until I uncover what's hidden in this setup.

So I journey on, with hope in my heart,
Through darkened caves, and realms apart.
The mystery of Minecraft is my quest,
To unlock its secrets, and put my mind at rest.

~ Arul Shah

Tales

CREEPERS

It's a full moon night, a normal Minecraft night. You are traveling between the trees to your houses, after chopping some wood. You were just reaching your house but,

Suddenly

You heard someone sneaking towards you, close, closer, and BOOM!

*You were blown up by a Creeper *

RESPAWN

You don't even know that this creeper has not just destroyed your Minecraft build but many. Most of you would have been told that the creeper is a result of a programming mistake in the game.

The developers were trying to make a pig mob but instead made the terrifying creeper just by MISTAKE.

Just think about it once, have you ever seen a creeper attacking any other mob?

Or Iron golems attack creepers.

The clear answer is NO!

But why do they attack only one player?

After a lot of research, I have found the answers.
Talking about creepers it's just a naturally occurring mob such as sheep,

pigs, and cows but the main difference here is,

They only attack the players, because you would not have seen any creeper attacking a villager or Iron Golem.

But the main point here is that the creeper has a goal.

What is the goal?

The story of the terrifying creeper starts from here, as you would be knowing Steve and Alex belong to an ancient human race that ruled the world of Minecraft and were richer than us and more advanced than we ever thought of them. But there is a problem which is that they are no longer in power.

One more human race we can find in the world which we can find now also in the world are villagers.

They just want to live in the village without any tension of using natural products.

But, our players Steve and Alex have the full right of building or destroy any monument or nature for their use.

Because of this, the ancient people in Minecraft made those explosive and terrifying creepers.

The main mission of the ancient people was to protect their land and monuments from being destroyed by players.

But,
As told in this story, they had pet cats because they wanted to protect themselves from creepers too.

So if players want to protect themselves or their building from getting destroyed they must opt for the values given by the ancient people of Minecraft which are to keep cats as their pets and around their buildings from getting destroyed as creepers are scared of cats.

WITCH

If we talk about the story of the witch it isn't a story, but an emotion or a story of sacrifice. If we look at it,it doesn't feel too dangerous ans aggressive mob.

Just try to match the face and looks of the Minecraft witch with the Minecraft villagers.

You'll find something in common like the long nose and hands in sleeves.

The Minecraft witch does not spawn anywhere in the world but has a specific spawn point which is the swamp hut.

In this hut, you'll find a crafting table, a cauldron, and A BLACK CAT!

Most of you would be considering witch as a hostile mob, which she is
But,

She never tries to attack the villagers instead Iron golems attack her, and if we think of witches as a threat to them.

If you would locate a biome known as icy tundra you will find an igloo in any random
place while roaming in the biome.

When you would see some grey carpets inside the igloo and if you break the white carpet in the middle of an igloo you'll see something Unbelievable.

You'll find a deep hole in the surface and when you go down through the hole beneath the surface. You would find a zombie villager inside who would be trapped!
And in the chests, you'll find a potion of weakness and a golden apple.

Now if we would add all of these clues together we would find the story of the witch.

Now, as you have read the clues let's start the **story**………

The story of the witch starts when the witch was not a witch first but a professional cleric villager. She was peacefully living in the village with other villagers but there was a problem which was that every full moon night all the zombies would attack the village. They tried to break the doors of the villager's houses and transformed many villagers into zombie villagers.

You can find proof of this incident by visiting the abandoned villages in Minecraft which can be considered old places where the witch first lived.

The cleric was so angry with this problem, that she made a promise to resolve it. She went to a biome known as icy_tundra and built an igloo for curing this problem.

You can find that curing chamber by visiting the icy_tundra igloo in your Minecraft worlds.
Now, if you want to visit the biome use the code below and explore that chamber by searching for the igloo.

<u>Code</u> - /locate biome minecraft:icy_tundra

After a lot of research and hard work, she finally discovered the cure for this problem and invited the chief and guards of her village to show her the cure.

After hearing this the chief thought that she was doing wrong to the villagers by trapping them and doing experiments.

Due to this, the chief told Iron golems and other villagers about the experiment and ordered the golems to attack her if she comes or enters the village again.

As she was not able to enter the village again, she built a swamp hut in the swamp biome and tamed a cat to be her friend.

This was the story of the cat that is found in the swamp hut of the witch.

and, if you want to visit the swamp biome and want to find the hut use the code.

<u>Code</u>

For visiting the swamp biome

/locate biomeminecraft:swamp_forest

For visiting the swamp hut

/locate structure Minecraft:swamp_hut
<u>How she came in pillager raids?</u>

One day, she was roaming in the search of new herbs and shrubs for making a potion.
Some pillagers saw her and invited her to their base.

The pillagers listened to her story about how she was thrown out of the village.

They were smart enough for making a deal with the witch to destroy villages.

They said:
"Hey! Witch you can be in our team so we can together take revenge for this behavior."

But, after all, she said:
"No! My goal is not to harm the villagers as it's not their fault but, I can help you to achieve your mission by providing healing potions to your army in the war."

Both of them agreed to this deal and that is why it can be seen during raids with the pillagers but never attacks any villager.

SOUL SAND

Soul sand is a block that can be found in the nether on Minecraft.

It is a so mysterious block found in Minecraft itself that makes hundreds of questions and reasons for its presence in the game and this book too.

Like when you walk on this sand why does this make you so slow?

Have you ever wondered about this question?

Just imagine this as if this block is stopping you from moving forward and wants help from you and is trying to tell you something important for you to listen to.

If you are interested in knowing more about this block known as soul sand read further because in this chapter you are not just going to know about the mystery of soul sand but find the real truth behind the souls and mystery.

Okay, let's just clarify this…
Soul sand is a block of sand that is found in the nether of Minecraft but what's special about this is that this block contains the souls of the Minecraft mobs which were first roaming in the normal world of Minecraft but are now converted

to this block considered as soul sand you can conclude this theory from the name of the block.

Have you ever traveled on soul sand with your Minecraft boots enchanted with SOUL SPEED?

Many of you who would be playing this game for a while now would have traveled
But,

Have you ever thought about why it gives you more speed when you run on the soul sand blocks?
And
If you would turn back and see some small blue-colored things coming off or being released what you would not know is that these are the souls of Minecraft mobs which are being released when are

walking with those enchanted boots on the sand.

GHAST

These mobs known as Ghasts are found in the world of Minecraft considered the hell of Minecraft or the nether.

Ghast does not have a story in it, it has a question lying in it which makes the reader curious to think about its own story. But, the good part is that it has a short description for you to think about it.

Talking about Ghast also considered as the crying mob is found nether. It's not only a mob but a scream of all the souls present in the nether of the Minecraft world.

You can consider this mob as vessels filled with souls which try to attack the player with fireballs that the ghast throws.

When the ghast screams most of the player gets scared (if you are not, amazing!) because it's not only the ghast screaming but thousands of souls trapped in the nether which are filled with ghast as a mob.

Minecraft souls?

Minecraft souls which are being referred to in the story of ghast and the previous chapter are the ones of the mobs that are no more in the real world of Minecraft but are now trapped in the nether.

ENDERMAN

These tall creatures with long hands and legs considered Endermans by every player can be called the most mysterious mobs in the whole game not just because of their mysterious looks and teleportation power but the reason of their presence all over the world.

Just think to yourself do these creatures even look like they belong to the Minecraft world?

The clear answer is NO! They don't belong

But, then why are they present in the overworld?

It makes sense if they would be present in the end world as the End world is completely a different world itself so they can have their mobs but why in the overworld?

The simple answer to this question is that "they have evolved from the ancient race of Minecraft people."

If you would have read the story of Creeper in this book you must be known the ancient race of Minecraft which looked just like players today but their rule is no more now.

Okay let's clarify this

Understand it as if you are roaming in a Minecraft world and you found villagers in a village do they look similar in any case to our players?

No!

So, the answer I used "they have evolved from the ancient race of ancient Minecraft people" means that these endermans which you see roaming in this world are those ancient humans which have evolved to become endermans.

Story….

So basically you can find so many structures which can be built only by players like desert pyramids and abandoned mineshafts.

But,

What you never thought about is that you didn't build that so who built it?

The answer is the ancient humans which are described in the above lines.

Just try to check that when a zombie attacks a villager they, at last, become an infected zombie villager they don't just die.

Just think that this must have happened with the ancient Minecraft human race like there must have been a zombie apocalypse that resulted in the decline of the ancient Minecraft race.

Strongholds….

If you would go on the internet and search for the meaning of Stronghold you will find the meaning as
"a place which is strongly built and difficult   to   attack."

So just, relate this meaning of stronghold from the above meaning given of the real stronghold.
So think it like there must be a zombie apocalypse in ancient times and the ancient humans must have thought to build another dimension to live in as the overworld was destroyed but the zombie apocalypse.

The new dimensions…..

The new decision which is going to be uncovered must be known by many of you
which is the "THE END"

The humans didn't want to go to that dimension but the situations made them go there.

When they went into the END dimension, they saw that the place was just like their dimension but divided into several small islands.

They had no other choice other than to survive there.

As the food consumption got low some humans started eating chorus fruit and as they ate it for a long time some of them started transforming into these creatures called…
Endermans.

And as the fruit became popular among the humans all of them started eating the fruit and all of them are now known as Endermans.

END (dimension)
+
MANS(people)
=
ENDERMANS
(people of end dimension)

The truth.....

So those of you who had been playing this game for a while and have encountered Endermans in front of you,

Must have heard the noise which they make but have you ever heard them carefully?

When you would hear them carefully you will understand that they want to talk to us!

(If you want to know how you can check those sounds you can go on the author's YouTube channel which is given at the beginning of the book)

Some words which endermans try to say are:

1) Hello!
2) Hi!
3) What's up?
4) Hey!
5) Thank you!

And one of the most mysterious sounds you can listen is "Look for the eye!"

From this phrase, the endermans try to convey to you that you have to look for the ender eye so that you can find the stronghold and activate it.

They just want help from you so that you can free them from the rule of the Ender dragon.

PHANTOM

The world of Minecraft is full of mysteries, but none are quite as terrifying as the phantom mob.

These ghostly creatures roam the land, haunting players and causing chaos wherever they go.

For years, players have tried to unravel the mysteries surrounding the phantom mob, but many questions remain unanswered.

 In this story, we will explore some of the most common mysteries surrounding the phantom mob and attempt to solve them.

What is the phantom mob?

A phantom mob is a group of ghostly creatures that

appear in Minecraft. They are known for their eerie

appearance and their ability to swoop down from the sky and attack players.

Some players believe that the phantom mob is the result of a curse or dark magic, while others speculate that they are the ghosts of fallen warriors.

What is the phantom membrane used for?

One of the most mysterious items in Minecraft is the phantom membrane.

This item is dropped by the phantom mob when it is defeated, but its purpose is unclear. Some players believe that the phantom membrane can be used to craft powerful weapons or armor, while others think that it is simply a useless item.

How do you avoid the phantom mob?

Avoiding the phantom mob can be a challenge, but there are a few strategies that players can use to stay safe. One of the most effective strategies is to stay indoors at night and avoid going outside until morning.

If you must go outside at night, be sure to have a weapon and be prepared to defend yourself.

What is the best way to defeat the phantom mob?

Defeating the phantom mob can be a challenge, but there are a few strategies that players can use to increase their chances of success.

One effective strategy is to use a bow and arrow to attack the phantom mob from a distance.

Another strategy is to use a sword to attack the phantom mob up close.

In conclusion, the phantom mob of Minecraft remains one of the most mysterious and terrifying creatures in the game. While there is still much that is unknown about these ghostly creatures, players can use the strategies outlined in this story to stay safe and increase their chances of defeating the phantom mob.

Whether you are a seasoned Minecraft player or a newcomer to the game, the phantom mob is sure to

keep you on the edge of your seat with its thrilling
mix of suspense, thrill, and horror.

GUARDIAN

The Guardian Temple is a mysterious and dangerous place located deep in the ocean in the game Minecraft. It is made up of solid prismarine blocks and is illuminated with an eerie blue glow. It is believed that the temple is home to a creature known as the Guardian, a giant squid-like creature with spiny tentacles and glowing blue eyes.

Many players have tried to explore the temple and uncover its secrets, but few have succeeded. The Guardian and its minions, small fish-like creatures, attack anyone who tries to enter the temple. The Guardian is incredibly powerful, with impossible to break armor and deadly attacks. Some players believe that the Guardian is immortal and has been protecting the temple for centuries.

Despite the danger, some players are still determined to uncover the secrets of the temple. They gather together and embark on a dangerous journey, fighting off the Guardian's minions and eventually facing the creature itself.

The Guardian Temple is a topic of discussion and speculation among

Minecraft players. Some believe that the temple was built by a long-forgotten civilization as a tribute to the Guardian, while others think that it was used for dark magic rituals. There are even rumors that there is something valuable hidden within its walls.

Entering the temple is not easy. The Guardian's minions swarm around the temple in large groups, attacking anyone who tries to enter. Those who manage to defeat them will then face the Guardian itself. Many players have attempted to defeat the Guardian, but few have succeeded. Its attacks are powerful and deadly, and its armor seems impossible to break.

Despite the challenge, there are still those who are determined to uncover the secrets of the temple. They gather together and embark on a dangerous journey, fighting off the Guardian's minions and eventually facing the creature itself. The journey is long and dangerous, but the reward for succeeding is great.

The Guardian Temple remains a mystery, but for those brave enough to explore its depths, it holds the promise of untold riches and knowledge. It is a challenge that only the bravest and most skilled Minecraft players can hope to conquer.

BLAZE

Blazes are one of the most fearsome and dangerous mobs in Minecraft, and their fiery attacks can easily take down even the most skilled player. But for those who are willing to take on the challenge, defeating Blazes can be a lucrative endeavor. In this story, we'll take a closer look at these fiery foes and explore some strategies for taking them down.

Blazes are found exclusively in the Nether, a dangerous and inhospitable dimension filled with lava flows, dangerous terrain, and other deadly mobs. They spawn in Blaze Spawners, which are found inside Nether Fortresses. To locate a Blaze Spawner, players must navigate through the Nether, avoiding hazards such as lava flows and magma cubes.

Once a Blaze Spawner is located, players must then take on the Blazes that spawn from it. Blazes are highly aggressive and will attack any player within their line of sight. They shoot fireballs at their targets, which can cause significant damage and set them on fire.

To defeat Blazes, players must first take precautions to protect themselves. This includes wearing fire-resistant armor such as a full set of Netherite or Diamond Armor, carrying a shield, and carrying fire resistance potions.

In addition to protective measures, players must also have a plan of attack. One effective strategy is to build a Blaze farm, which is a structure designed to trap and kill Blazes automatically. Blaze farms can be built using a variety of materials, such as Nether Brick or Obsidian.

Another strategy is to engage Blazes from a distance using ranged weapons such as bows and arrows or crossbows. This can be particularly effective if players have enchanted weapons, such as the Flame or Power enchantments.

Regardless of the strategy chosen, taking on Blazes requires patience, skill, and the right equipment. Players should also be prepared to face other hazards in the Nether, such as lava flows, magma cubes, and other dangerous mobs.

But for those who are successful in defeating Blazes, the rewards can be significant. Blazes drop Blaze Rods, which are valuable items that can be used to craft potions and other useful items. They also drop experience points, which can be used to level up the player's character.

In addition to their value as a source of loot, defeating Blazes can also be a source of pride and satisfaction for Minecraft players. Taking down one of the most fearsome and dangerous mobs in the game requires skill, strategy, and bravery.

In conclusion, Blazes are a formidable opponent in Minecraft, but with the right preparation and strategy, they can be defeated. Whether building a Blaze farm or engaging them from a distance with ranged weapons, taking on Blazes requires patience, skill, and the right equipment. But for those who are willing to take on the challenge, the rewards can be significant, both in terms of loot and personal satisfaction.

SKELETON

Skeletons are one of the most common mobs in Minecraft, found in nearly every biome and often encountered during the day and night. They are a formidable enemy that can deal significant damage to unprepared players, but they also provide a valuable source of loot and experience points. In this story, we'll take a closer look at Skeletons and explore strategies for defeating them.

Skeletons are mobs that are armed with a bow and arrow, making them a ranged enemy. They have the ability to shoot arrows at players from a distance, and they are also capable of small attacks when players get too close. Skeletons are especially dangerous when encountered in groups, as they can coordinate their attacks and quickly defeat players.

To defeat Skeletons, players must first be prepared with the right equipment. This includes wearing armor such as Iron or Diamond Armor, carrying a shield, and carrying ranged weapons such as a bow and arrow or a crossbow. Enchanted weapons and armor can also be particularly effective against Skeletons, especially those with the

Bane of Arthropods or Smite enchantments.

Once players are properly equipped, they can engage Skeletons in a variety of ways. One strategy is to attack from a distance using ranged weapons, such as a bow and arrow or a crossbow. This can be particularly effective if players have enchanted weapons, as the arrows can deal additional damage.

Another strategy is to engage Skeletons in small attacks combat. Players can use a sword or axe to deal damage to Skeletons when they get close, while a shield can be used to block arrows and protect against small attacks.

In addition to combat strategies, players can also use environmental factors to their advantage. Skeletons are susceptible to fire and sunlight, and players can use fire-based weapons or sunlight to deal additional damage. Players can also use terrain features to their advantage, such as using obstacles to block arrows and small attacks.

Regardless of the strategy chosen, defeating Skeletons requires patience and skill. Players must be prepared to dodge arrows, block attacks, and avoid getting defeated by groups of Skeletons. They must also be prepared to face other hazards in Minecraft, such as other hostile mobs, environmental hazards, and terrain obstacles.

But for those who are successful in defeating Skeletons, the rewards can be significant. Skeletons drop valuable loot, including bones and arrows, which can be used to craft other items or used in combat. They also drop experience points, which can be used to level up the player's character and unlock new abilities.

In conclusion, Skeletons are a common enemy in Minecraft that require skill and strategy to defeat. Whether engaging them from a distance using ranged weapons or engaging in small attacks combat, players must be prepared with the right equipment and tactics. But for those who are successful, defeating Skeletons can be a valuable source of loot and experience points, and a source of pride and satisfaction for Minecraft players.

ENDER DRAGON

In the game of Minecraft, the Enderdragon is a creature that is both feared and revered. It is the final boss that players must defeat to win the game, and it guards the End, a mysterious and dangerous dimension. But the Enderdragon is more than just a monster. It holds the key to unlocking some of the game's greatest mysteries and secrets, and it has a rich and fascinating history.

Long ago, there was an ancient human race in Minecraft that had a deep understanding of the game's magic. They might have been the first ones to discover the Enderdragon and its power. They understood that the Enderdragon was a powerful guardian of the End, meant to protect its secrets and power. They also knew that the dragon's power was dangerous and had to be used carefully, to prevent it fall into the wrong hands.

However, there was also an evil group called the Obsidian Cult that wanted to control the power of the Enderdragon for their own selfish purposes. They believed they could use its power to change the Minecraft universe in their own way. They were a threat to the game, and it was up to someone to stop them.

As the player explored the secrets of the End and the Enderdragon, they found clues about the ancient human race and the Obsidian Cult. They discovered a mysterious artifact that was connected to the Enderdragon's power, and they knew that it held the key to unlocking some of the greatest mysteries of Minecraft. But they also uncovered a darker side to the Enderdragon's power. Some of the ancient human race had become obsessed with the dragon's power and had tried to use it to control and manipulate others. They had even attempted to harness the dragon's power to create new, dangerous creatures to serve them.

The player knew that they had to act fast to stop the Obsidian Cult from unleashing destruction upon the game. They were following in the footsteps of the ancient human race, using their knowledge to protect the Minecraft universe. They were up against powerful forces that would stop at nothing to protect their secrets. But the player was determined to uncover the truth about the Enderdragon's power, and to ensure that it was used for good, rather than for evil.

In the end, the player discovered that the artifact was the key to unlocking a portal that led to a secret realm, where the true power of the Enderdragon was revealed. They found themselves face to face with the dragon itself, and were filled with a sense of awe and reverence. They knew that they had uncovered one of the greatest mysteries of Minecraft, and that they had a responsibility to use their knowledge to protect the game and its universe.

The player realized that the Enderdragon was not just a monster, but a powerful guardian of the End with ancient magic. They learned that the ancient human race had a deep understanding of the game's magic and might have discovered the Enderdragon. They understood that the Obsidian Cult wanted to control the Enderdragon's power for their own selfish reasons, but it could be harnessed for good to protect the Minecraft universe. They were determined to protect the game and its secrets, following in the footsteps of the ancient human race.

The player spent many days exploring the secrets of the End and the Enderdragon, and they discovered many mysteries that were hidden from plain sight. They learned about the ancient portals that led to the End and the mysterious creatures that lived there. They studied the symbols that were etched into the ancient stone tablets and converted their meaning. They even discovered hidden temples that were dedicated to the Enderdragon and its power.

Through their journey, the player came to understand that Minecraft was more than just a game. It was a universe full of secrets and mysteries that were still

unexplored.

PIGLINS

Long ago, there was an ancient human race in Minecraft that had a deep understanding of the game's magic. In Minecraft, the Piglins are a unique and fascinating mob that live in the Nether dimension. They are known for their love of gold, hostile behavior towards unprepared players, and unique culture and history. Understanding the Piglins' behavior and customs can help players navigate the dangerous Nether dimension and uncover secrets about the game's universe.

The Piglins' love of gold is not just mere greed; it has a magical property that they can use to craft powerful weapons and tools. They also worship a god known as the Piglin King and are afraid of the Nether's other inhabitants. The Piglins are part of an ancient civilization that once flourished in the Nether, building great cities and temples dedicated to gods of fire and lava. However, a cataclysmic event destroyed their cities and temples, causing the Piglins to turn hostile.

Players who explore the Nether's ancient ruins can uncover clues about the Piglins' past and even discover a powerful artifact that's connected to their magic. Additionally, Piglin Brutes are a more aggressive variant of the regular Piglin mob. They are tougher and more dangerous, but they drop valuable items upon defeat.

The Piglins also have unique interactions with other mobs and items. For example, they will trade gold ingots for various items, such as Obsidian, Soul Sand, and Netherite Scrap. They also become aggressive towards players who open chests or mine blocks in their presence, unless the player is wearing gold armor.

Furthermore, Piglins can be distracted by thrown gold items, allowing players to sneak past them undetected. They will also attack Hoglins on sight, a hostile mob that can be found in the Nether.

Overall, the Piglins offer a unique challenge for players exploring the Nether. Understanding their culture and history can lead to uncovering even greater secrets and give players a better understanding of the game's lore.

PILLAGER

Deep in the heart of the forest, there was a village that had been plagued by pillagers for years. The villagers had tried everything to stop them, but nothing seemed to work. They had built walls, hired guards, and even prayed to the gods for help. But still, the pillagers came, stealing their crops and livestock, and leaving destruction in their wake.

One day, a wise old man came to the village. He had traveled far and wide, and had seen many things that most people could not even imagine. The villagers saw hope in him, and asked for his help in dealing with the pillagers. The old man agreed, but only on one condition – that they follow his instructions exactly.

The villagers agreed, and the old man began his work. He asked for a small group of volunteers, and together they set out into the forest, deep into the territory of the pillagers. They traveled for days, until they came to a clearing where the pillagers were camped.

The old man and his volunteers watched the pillagers for days, studying their movements, and learning their ways. They discovered that the pillagers were led by a powerful leader, a man who was feared by all who knew him. He was known only as "The Raven", and he wore a cloak of black feathers that made him appear as though he had wings.

The old man knew that if they were to defeat the pillagers, they must first defeat The Raven. He devised a plan, and the volunteers set to work. They gathered together all the resources they could find – wood, stone, metal, and anything else that could be used as a weapon.

They worked day and night, building traps and weapons, and training themselves in the art of warfare. The old man instructed them on the ways of the forest, teaching them how to move quietly and avoid detection. He told them stories of battles he had fought in, and of the strategies he had used to emerge victorious.

Finally, the day came when they were ready. The old man led them into battle, and they fought with all their might. The pillagers were taken by surprise, and they fought back fiercely. The battle was long and brutal, but in the end, the villagers emerged victorious. The Raven himself was defeated, and the pillagers were forced to flee.

The villagers celebrated their victory, and they hailed the old man as a hero. They asked him how he had known how to defeat the pillagers, and he smiled enigmatically. "It was no mystery," he said. "It was simply a matter of understanding your enemy, and using that knowledge to your advantage."

And so, the village was never plagued by pillagers again. The old man stayed for a time, teaching the villagers all he knew, and then he disappeared as suddenly as he had come. But his lessons lived on, and the villagers passed them down from generation to generation, so that they would never forget the greatest mystery of pillaging – that knowledge is the key to victory.

WANDERING

TRADER

The Wandering Trader and the Unemployable Villager may seem like minor characters in the vast world of Minecraft, but they are integral to the game's lore and offer a unique perspective on the struggles of outcasts.

The Unemployable Villager's bug in the game is not the only issue that plagues them. They are often shunned by other villagers and treated as outsiders. This has led some players to speculate that the Unemployable Villager may have been cursed by a powerful wizard or witch, causing them to be rejected by their own kind.

The Wandering Trader, on the other hand, is believed to have been cursed by the Enderdragon. According to legend, the Wandering Trader made a deal with the dragon in exchange for a rare item, but was cursed to roam the world for eternity as a result. While this may seem like a fictional story, many players have reported encountering the cursed trader and hearing their sad tale.

Despite their hardships, both the Wandering Trader and the Unemployable Villager have found ways to thrive in the Minecraft world. The Wandering Trader's ability to acquire rare items makes them a valuable resource for players, while the Unemployable Villager's inability to be assigned a job has made them a sought-after collector's item for some players.

In a world where players often focus on building, mining, and battling, the stories of the Wandering Trader and the Unemployable Villager add a much-needed element of mystery and fascinate. They remind players that there is more to the game than just the mechanics, and that even the smallest characters can have a big impact on the Minecraft world.

So next time you encounter a Wandering Trader or an Unemployable Villager in your Minecraft world, take a moment to appreciate their unique story and the struggles they face. Who knows, maybe you'll be the one to finally break the Wandering Trader's curse or find a way to assign a job to the Unemployable Villager.

DROWNED

The Drowned is a unique mob in Minecraft that is related to the Zombie. It is often found in bodies of water, and can be a challenging opponent for players to face.

Similar to Zombies, Drowned mobs are undead creatures that are hostile towards players. However, unlike Zombies, Drowned mobs are more powerful in water, able to move quickly and deal significant damage to players.

One theory about the origins of Drowned mobs is that they were once Zombies who drowned in bodies of water, and were subsequently transformed into their current form. This theory is supported by the fact that Drowned mobs often drop Zombie-related items, such as Rotten Flesh and Zombie Heads.

Despite their similarities to Zombies, Drowned mobs have unique abilities that make them a formidable opponent. They are able to swim quickly and deal damage with their tridents, making them particularly dangerous in bodies of water.

Players must be cautious when encountering Drowned mobs, as they can easily defeat an unprepared player. It is recommended to have a good supply of weapons and armor, as well as the ability to move quickly and efficiently in water.

In addition to their combat abilities, Drowned mobs also have a unique ability to pick up and wield underwater items, such as tridents and fishing rods. This adds an element of surprise and challenge to encounters with Drowned mobs, as players must be prepared for unexpected attacks.

Despite their fearsome reputation, Drowned mobs also add an element of mystery and fascinate to the Minecraft world. Players are always looking for new ways to uncover the secrets of the game and discover the origins of these unique creatures.

ENDERMITE

Endermites are tiny creatures found in the Minecraft world that spawn when an Enderman teleports. They are often seen as a nuisance and are easily squished by players. However, these little critters have a mysterious side that many players may not be aware of.

Legend has it that Endermites are created when Endermen use their teleportation powers to travel to other dimensions. During these journeys, some of the Enderman's teleportation energy is left behind, which forms into Endermites.

Despite their small size, Endermites are capable of causing chaos in the Minecraft world. They can attract the attention of nearby Endermen, causing them to teleport to the Endermite's location. This can be a useful strategy for players looking to lure Endermen into traps or away from areas where they may cause damage.

But Endermites are not just a tool for players to use. Some players believe that these creatures may hold the key to unlocking the mysteries of the End dimension, where the Enderdragon resides. It's said that if enough Endermites are gathered in one place, they can create a portal to the End, allowing players to enter the dimension and face the Enderdragon.

While this theory has yet to be proven, it adds to the fascinate and mystery surrounding these tiny creatures. Some players even speculate that Endermites may have a greater purpose in the Minecraft world, one that has yet to be uncovered.

Despite their small stature, Endermites play an important role in the Minecraft world. Whether they are a nuisance or a key to unlocking mysteries, players will continue to encounter these creatures on their adventures in the game.

THE MYSTERY

ISN'T FINISHED

NEXT PART

SOON !

THOUGHTS

After reading this book you must be having some questions about the mysteries discussed in this book, write those here so you can show these **GREAT** mysteries in front of your friends which you are solving...

Happy
Minecrafting